PRESENTED BY

Jack Van Slyke

fly

Jump

run

Read

scream

William Denning

2005

SMYTHE GAMBRELL LIBRARY • WESTMINSTER SCHOOLS

We were forty miles from Albany.

Forget it I never shall.

When we first set sail to carry the mail

On the E-ri-e Canal,

On the E-ri-e Canal.

To Julie and Sam
–E. A. K.

Back at Eric, with thanks
–A. G.

Text copyright © 2002 by Eric A. Kimmel • Illustrations copyright © 2002 by Andrew Glass
All Rights Reserved
Printed in the United States of America
First Edition
www.holidayhouse.com

Library of Congress Cataloging-in-Publication Data
Kimmel, Eric A.
The Erie Canal pirates / by Eric Kimmel ; illustrated by Andrew Glass.—1st ed.
p. cm.
Summary: A boat captain and his men battle Bill McGrew and his pirate crew on the Erie Canal in a rhyming tale inspired by a folksong.
ISBN 0-8234-1657-7 (hardcover)
[1. Pirates–Fiction. 2. Boats and boating–Fiction. 3. Erie Canal (N.Y.)–Fiction. 4. Stories in rhyme.] I. Glass, Andrew, 1949– ill. II. Title.
PZ8.3.K5595 Er 2002
[E]–dc21   2001059428

Designed by Trish P. Watts

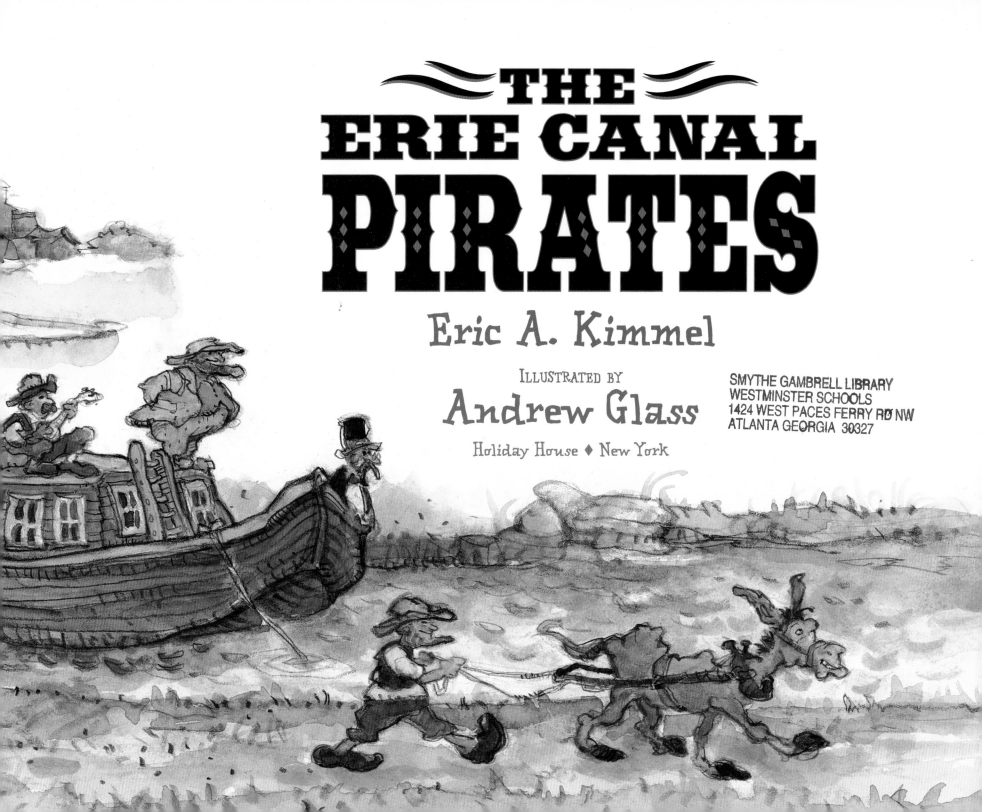

~THE~
ERIE CANAL
PIRATES

Eric A. Kimmel

ILLUSTRATED BY

Andrew Glass

Holiday House ◆ New York

We had just pulled out of Mohawk.
Captain Flynn had set the sail.
And on the bank our mule, Old Frank,
Hee-hawed and flicked his tail,
Hee-hawed and flicked his tail.

We spied a boat to windward,
Coming upon us fast.
The lookout cried, "Ahoy! She flies
Jolly Roger from her mast!
Jolly Roger from her mast!"

The boat pulled up alongside,
And the sight filled us with woe.
It was Bill McGrew and his pirate crew,
The Terror of Buffalo,
The Terror of Buffalo.

But Captain Flynn was a fighter,
And the crew meant to keep their pay.
And Frank the Mule wouldn't let those cruel
Pirates steal his hay,
Cruel pirates steal his hay.

So we ran out all our cannon,
Loaded with shot and ball.
And we fired a blast that could be heard past
Saratoga to Montreal,
Saratoga to Montreal.

Pirates swung down from the rigging.
They outnumbered us ten to one.
With pistol and sword they swarmed aboard
For the battle had just begun,

The battle

had just begun.

We brawled from Canajoharie,
From Ilion to Liverpool.
While good Old Frank scuffled on the bank
With a one-eyed pirate mule,
A one-eyed pirate mule.

Captain steered us north at Fairport
Into Lake Ontario.
"It's the long way round but I'll bring us down
To the dock at Buffalo,
To the dock at Buffalo."

We heard a sudden roaring,
Like a thousand bugle calls.
"There's no way through!" cried Bill McGrew.
"We're headed for Niagara Falls!

We're headed

Two boats swept into the whirlpool
Without any way to stop.
Captain Flynn declared, "Boys, don't be scared.
I'll take us to the top.

I'll take us to the top."

The current knocked us sideways.
We hollered out screams and bawls.
But Captain steered by the set of Frank's ears.
And he sailed us up the Falls,
Right up Niagara Falls.

Alas! Those Erie pirates
Were never to be seen no more.
Their ghosts walk around with the dead and the drowned
On the Tonawanda shore,
On the Tonawanda shore.

In Buffalo they shouted,
"Captain Flynn has saved the day!"
So they toasted our crew with a bumper or two,
And Frank got a bale of hay.
Old Frank got a bale of hay.

We were forty miles from Albany.

Forget it I never shall.

So turn around, men, and we'll do it again

On the E-ri-e Canal,

On the E-ri-e Canal.

AUTHOR'S NOTE

As a native New Yorker, I grew up singing the original Erie Canal song: "We were forty miles from Albany./Forget it I never shall./What a terrible storm we had that night/On the E-ri-e Canal,/On the E-ri-e Canal."

The Erie Canal is a long ditch that was built in the early nineteenth century to connect the Great Lakes with the port of New York. The canal is one of the greatest achievements of American engineering, considering that it was built without power tools or professional engineers. Pick and shovel laborers, mostly Irish immigrants, dug every mile by hand.

The idea for writing my own version of the Erie Canal song came to me while I was visiting a school in Fairport, New York. One of the teachers told me she had taken her class on a field trip to a restored tavern along the canal as part of their Erie Canal unit. I asked if she had told them about the pirates.

I then proceeded to spin a yarn about buccaneers lurking along the tow path and fierce battles that the "canawlers" fought with them. The teachers quickly realized I was making it up. Even so, they all agreed that an Erie Canal pirate story was a great idea.

To tell the tale, however, I had to take a few liberties with geography. The only way to get from Fairport to Lake Ontario is to go overland. And while there are individuals who survived going over Niagara Falls, no one to my knowledge has ever succeeded in going up.